Brown Sugar Baby

by 'Trell The Poet

Brown Sugar Baby

Message to myself,

You are enough.

You are growing.

You are progressing.

You are light.

Keep evolving, Ma'.

-Trell

Table of Content

Welcome, brown sugar babies!

I write to inspire others and to encourage them to speak their truth. These poems are written for you. This tale is my true story, but I know you'll be able to relate. Here's my everlasting journey.

"No human being can be more human than another human being. You can be finer. You can be prettier, but you can't be more human."

-Dr. Maya Angelou

Des'Trell

I am

the queen of imperfection.

The big face,

wide nose,

brown skin,

African hair, and

5 feet formed of satisfaction.

With an edgy smile that cocks crooked,

cracking at the concrete eyes of the owl

reflecting on my confidence.

See,

I wear my crown with pride.

Laying out all my flaws in my own royal state

and only heaven hate can reflect on my character,

refusing to open the gates to a new chapter.

See,

I wear my crown with a smile

cause only God knows the struggle in balancing this heavy

metal

and while these stones are being thrown at my feet,

I rise to every occasion

With the determination to succeed

cause see,

I am a queen that knows her worth.

And with every opportunity,

I snatch the crown, owning my position in confidence.

I catch the sound of optimism.

Speaking of hopes and faith,

I catch the sound of ambition in my wisdom.

And speaking of wisdom,

this maturity has cost me to be

a developing young lady.

Seeking respect from within since without doesn't matter,

like without your touch, my makeup becomes unattractive.

That's

not

a

factor.

And seeking respect from within

has changed me;

shaped me

and rather than begging for your acceptance,

I'll ignore your judgements

cause I am a queen

and a woman in the making.

And speaking of making, under God's blessings
I'll cherish every moment while living and creating a
legacy.
And speaking of legacy,
I pray that every young lady looks in the mirror and
notices a legend because we are all queens.
And speaking of queens,
I
am
a
queen.

T.

Comfort Zone

In this notebook

this pad

on this paper

unwritten sentences

vowels in love and curiosity

 Life spent with this ink

 tattooed emotions

unexplained thoughts

secrets

unvoiced opinions

 hidden scars

In this

 with this

 on this

for this tattooed heart

expression comes loud

emotions based upon disappointments

 so, in this notebook

 I am

 I feel

 I become free

escaping from what they think of me

My confidence

My cage

My mind has opened up

My soul

My heart

My head has raised up

So, I am

I feel

I become

She with her head held high

A strong spine in her back, a firm attitude,

Knowledge, the intelligence attached.

In this room

with the company of a rocking chair

dancing to the music of freedom, the beat beneath

my feet takes full advantage

so I am

I feel

I become

Me

on ten toes.

T.

19/11/06

Sometimes I wonder where life is taking me, everybody does. Even when we feel like we know, there's always an unknown; Always another surprise. Creations form from inspired human beings in a room full of inspired human beings. A vibrant spirit feeding off positive energy and peace finds me in the middle of chaos, in mid-air. Calming breezes rush my UV waves, strengthening the abundance within my atmosphere. Motivation pulls me back with patience and purpose. Sometimes I wonder about their purposes, possessing an evolutionary momentum while sitting in satisfaction. I have come so far; mentally, physically, and emotionally. Allowing myself to refocus due to the setbacks and disappointments that I won't engage in dwelling on. No one knows what the future holds, but negativity can leach on forever. We shall not speak into existence of what cannot be blessed, but what can be saved and as we continue to live and learn, we find new discoveries and new meanings.

T.

Sticky tongues roll over on
cloudy minds and closed eyes.
Tangled thoughts overthinking love,
overthinking the unthinkable that is inevitable,
insanely sinking in naked grass.
Weary tears tears bad habits of a weary woman
overshadowed by gloomy smiles
and these sticky tongues know secrets unwritten like the
four walls in my bedroom.
These sticky tongues are the only ones I could fully
convide in.
Self reflecting in the mirror
hotboxing the bathroom
and all I see is me besides these locs,
beyond this bad brown bitch;
still connecting the dots of a soulful young woman.
These sticky tongues hold the heavy heart beneath these
pupils pierced with superior fate.
Flawed and all, I hold my weight and I won't fold.

T.

Young Love

Back then

I was searching for something,

                    no clue of what the fuck that was,

like being kids in the court way with adrenaline rushing.

Hormones aspirating, like butterflies in my stomach.

Hearts was all over the world in my eyes,

13 having wet dreams about

Chris Brown.

First crush,

crushed my expectations after I caught my first nut.

And back then,

I was searching for love.

                    No clue of what the fuck that was,

looking for love in the wrong niggas like,

these niggas ain't shit, but

it's just a choice.

Unlatched hearts walked ceilings like elephants at home.

                               Home,

where the heart lies underneath footsteps tracking scars.

Lost trails.

Trynna' find my way back,

way back when innocence was
 still,
but silver spoons weren't in the cabinets.
My mama heart was colder than the leftovers in the fridge
and I hate it. How to love,
if it was never brought to your attention
to dimension in- between these walls so tight;
an empress
jewel pyramid upon stones,

                        a dime
                  a dollar can't buy.

I've felt in love a couple times, but haven't been in love yet
        I've felt a love I could never replace and
              a love I would love to erase.
How to love
with a numb heart, cold blooded.
        Distant lover and I can't let you get to close cause hurt
                    people, hurt people.
How to love
when you never really knew love before?
I thought love was perfect, but really
 love is pure.

T.

The trees whistle at the sound of

life racing,

love bleeding,

and time cheating its way.

Crashing,

hoping to survive

Trusting its speed while creating an unknown life,

hoping to survive.

In the woods near nature,

surrounded by its territory, you face danger.

War against hunger and thirst.

Bear.

Bear as to the struggle

Patience as to war.

This life became unknown to you,

where you knew

nothing;

had nothing,

and while life was becoming a rain, you

my sister chased it.

Thinking there's something, but really it's nothing.

See someone knew the lyrics to the tree's whistle, but only

hummed;

Embracing this unknown music,
only one knew.
But you, my sister knew nothing.
Life.
Love.
Living.
You knew nothing.
See, this someone flies through the forest with the danger,
The nature;
swims across the ocean with the sharks and the whales
with no fear.
warmness feels the veins,
embracing the knowledge of life,
but for you…
time has no patience,
living has no resistance,
and life has no wisdom.
When the trees whistle,
do you wonder why you hear silence or
feel empty.

T.

The White Shadow

I stepped over a puddle of pain,
not realizing my name was in vain of that reflection.
With my face structure and complexion
drawn by a rainbow, I stopped.
Stared,
And daydreamed about what happiness feels like.
I suddenly get a chill caused by a warm spirit,
with a gentle touch, rubbing my cheek.
My smile releases hidden scars that have no end.
I think.
I thought.
I counted every second I am contemplating on this journey,
I am destined to explore.
I think.
I thought.
I am sure that I am slowly finding myself.
I think.
I thought.
I am sure that you will eventually accept me, but if not
Who gives a fuck.

I am that poetic figure that carries an old soul,
making up for lost times and the whispers behind these
closed doors.
I am comfortable in my own skin.
I think.
I thought what if,
but within each second guess, I feel fear preparing me for
failure.
Well at least, I thought.
That fear that's growing deep in my heart, my soul is
fighting to reach my thoughts with its force.
I think.
I thought
you the baddest bitch.
I mean you not a dog, but you are a dog at this.
This humor of being yourself.
Fuck whose looking and judging your every move.
This is your mark.
Your passion.
That daydream of being a star,
write your name big as fuck with a permanent mark.
I am her.
The one that's stuck and scared of change, but her.

She's waiting to change what they wished for, fearing that
she will forget where she came from, see
I was born uptown of these New Orleans streets.
12 years old, my first high was offered to me.
Pregnant at 15,
confused and vulnerable for any dumb ass nigga to pay
attention to me.
Running round canal like it was fuckin Sesame Street, 16.
Intelligent, but naïve at the same time.
But now,
I am wiser and much more mature.
I am 19
chasing dreams that some are still dreaming, but I an
feening for a reality of destinies.
Feening for wisdom, knowledge of life.
Feening for the struggles to knock at my feet and determine
my strength
because I won't fall
at fear
and I won't fail
weak.
I think.
I thought facing fears forms a variety of accomplishments.

Twenty in April and I'm still not near the adulthood I
picture living, but I know some adults that has what I want
and still
get child played images.
Last night,
it stormed
and there was a bunch of puddles reflecting on my society,
reflecting a path where my footsteps have traveled and
moved forward
to become this unique someone, stepping out the rain.

T

Bittersweet Blessings

I imagine

the feeling of your warm skin

smooth, like black soap.

Flashbacks of your heartbeat,

sharing a significant harmony,

stuck with me.

Flashbacks of mama fussing at me;

confused me

caught up in some shit.

First love

became the first heartbreak.

Revenge roaming rivers up my alley.

Young, insecure me,

ignoring the fact that I barely knew this nigga,

virgin me, 15, foolish

to want him to feel the pain I carried.

Wish I knew what I know now,

feelings are temporary

and other than these lessons divined in me,

You are the only thing cherished.

T.

A young girl with little to no guidance can leave her running into lessons to learn with no one to get advice from. A lot of shit I couldn't talk to my mama about which made it uncomfortable to talk to her about anything. My sister and I didn't have a close relationship so I ran to my friends and sometimes niggas. Even my friends' mama. I was fifteen and sixteen years old, and curious about the world. My mama was there, but at times it was like she wasn't even there for the times I really needed her. I had to learn a lot on my own and make way for myself and at one point, it was too much that I felt like I couldn't handle it. As a child, you need your parents and you crave a love that can't nobody can fill, but you try to make them fit because the feeling feels similar. Some holes can't be repaired by what you desire and sometimes you have to heal yourself. It doesn't hit you until you are mature enough to understand and comprehend the complexities of life and some things are hard to learn and unlearn, but it is inevitable that that's required. Not everyone is dealt the same cards and some people might have a harder life than others, but we all can help and relate and give advice. Sometimes the best advice comes from within when you stop doubting yourself and trust your instincts. My mama says, "it takes a village to raise a child, "and I believe that because without those examples, I wouldn't be who I am.

T.

Dignified

I catch myself
Sometimes
 looking in the mirror, picking out my flaws and all in the
figure.
Disfigured.
Oh, maybe my waist ain't big enough,
Maybe
 my acne is not clearing up fast enough.
In this lifetime,
it's a must to do what it takes to one up and come up.
Losing yourself.
You confusing yourself,
speeding through life,
with your knees scrapping on cracked ice
you're abusing yourself.
I'll past.
Continuing in finding myself,
 using my talent,
 and owning my truth.
Embracing my flaws, I pause,
staring at this beautiful view.
The girl with the big nose,
shawty got a tempo,

give her a pen and your mind will explode as she spits flows;

Middle fingers up with her mic, like kudos.

Natural hair gone wild.

Beautiful black queen, confident in her own style.

The girl was born with big dreams, uniquely defined under a specific star.

Some can relate, but to the star

Maybe to her,

 but you didn't live within her to commit her.

See, we all have our own opposition

and even though we are all equally human,

                    our humor can be a little bit different.

Indifferent to those who wear their clothes differently.

She embraces all and encourage them to be committed,

in the midst of this "hater condition."

Consistent,

 locked with this pen placed in between her fingers;

Tangling her sentences,

 juggling her senses.

 She's committed,

recommending everyone to find passion in the dreams they are chasing

within all the manipulation.

Third eye open, surpassing the system's economic schemes.

Point taken.

Hearts shaking.

Minds wandering and wondering,

Running with every clue to see through temptation, but this life was built

upon stumbles and struggles,

surviving and sliding through these

 red lights, flash light.You past a stop sign, can't rewind.

You missed the opportunities chasing analogies.

These niggas ain't loyal, B.

These bitches be frauds,

flaunting material weaknesses.

Young queens with low self-esteem, you see.

T.

Mirror

I'll stand still

and let you analyze this picture taken,

filled with mistakes.

Lessons learned.

Flipping through memories way back,

when I used to look at you

for hours,

waiting for this page to turn.

When I thought that if I stared too hard,

you'll crack,

kicking glass metals in my eyes.

Permanently blind, but

in each minute,

I notice something

I hated.

I liked;

Maybe,

I noticed something I didn't noticed back then

when I used to watch you

for days.

And in every blue moon,

shooting stars glow, in the delay of this glo.

It just amazes me,

how in this day,

I am better than I was yesterday.

I'll use that picture taken to remind me

and since you haven't cracked yet,

I know that I am on the right track.

T.

A Declaration

A fractured heart needs a moment in peace

Alone

to reflect on the growing pains endured, time and time

again.

A fractured heart needs a moment to grow

and a moment might take a lil minute

to repair and gather what's been lost.

Pieces of my heart torn apart.

A fractured heart needs space

to fulfil the remedy of healing,

manifesting happiness over everything,

resonating with self-love

even more than before because before,

this fractured heart was lost

with just enough strength to not give up.

Done exposing my most sacred gold to those that take my

presence for granted.

Lately, I've been more selfish with myself because

a fractured heart needs a moment to release.

T.

20/02/23

Family is supposed to be your backbone when you feel like there's nothing else. Ideally, family is the ones who know you best, supports you at your worst, and always represents home. Some of us are fortunate to have that ideal bond and then we have my family, which is one out of many that can't get alone, can't keep calm, and very dysfunctional. When there's cycles being repeated for years and even the adults can fix it, you have to retrain yourself. Unlearning behaviors to make a peaceful life for your future. Experiencing domestic violence, verbal abuse, mental abuse, and anything else that toxicity can bring. You become immune to the system; family isn't perfect. Actually, nothing is perfect about life. Everything happens for a reason and you see people for who they really are. As you become into your own, you allow more that's in your control. Family is hard to love at a distance, but sometimes it costs your happiness if you don't.

T.

Living Under A Rock

I AM FREE…

With the thought of me being ugly

to you.

With the thought of not being enough,

when everyone and everything around you seems perfect

and easy

for you.

And at some point,

 I felt some sort of resentment because of you,

towards you, and anyone that vouched for you,

but with the person I have become,

I forgave you.

Forgave me for thinking that being angry will not only help

me make you feel me, but

just to put you in my shoes.

I AM FREE…

When my soul lives in the moment

and collaborate;

humbly saturated in purified satisfaction.

Numb to all this chaos of chit chattering birds,

Ignoring the ignorance before I get ignorant;

Using my strengths

before letting a bitch get under my skin.

Self-respect won't allow weak distractions.

When I take a moment and breathe

through each respiration, I feel internal happiness.

Not just because of any other aspirations

wished upon me, good and bad, but

Because of this spiritual healing of

becoming my own and knowing the known of the unknown

that I am still searching for.

I AM FREE…

With the mindset of not giving up

and not giving in

and not being sorry for who I am.

Accepting the growths and

changes I am faced with;

not listening to the naysayers,

hatred carries.

The foolish games, worn and played out.

The people that overlooked me and counted me out.

I am cleansing

from my childhood and teenage years.

From my mama's

drunken conversations about doodles,

to my father,

drugged out and damaged

or that biological vein,

sinking in a trench.

My sister and brothers

lost and trying to find their way back

to no beginning.

Me,

A child in loss of a child,

lost and running wild.

Everything that took a toll on my spiritual healing and

distracted me, but

helped me to see that

I am not perfect.

I am not to be seen and not heard,

not replaceable and won't be curved.

I am a star.   -in my own little way

I am human. -learning lessons and making mistakes

I am loved. -and its ok if it's not by you

I am free. -dedication to you

T.

Family Ties

As the message from me sends to the heavens above,

I pray that my great-grandma's soul will forever be loved.

I pray to god my grandma's heart won't be misunderstood,

and my mama's anxiety won't ever relive.

I pray my sister and brothers will hold hands with me.

I pray for god to have repent on this family.

21 years of distress.

Fights back to back.

Low blows, word of mouth.

Some shit you won't expect.

Some shit I even regret

because what is taught is bound to repeat again.

Mama depressed,

escaping to her only cave she knew best.

And after so many cans, the pain wore less.

And after so many years,

clusters clouding creases of

blood vein deep.

Same blood drawn from enemies,

devil tendencies.

Burning bridges,

 bricking walls between barriers of genuine love and

so called loyalty.

Misguided.

Morals vain deeper

cause even the ones closest to you could hit you where it

hurts.

Scars lies deeper than the grave with bodies covered like

mud baths burying

stilled grudges.

Communication slowly vanish with

 lack of courage to balance

and after so many headaches, nigga just throw the fuckin

towel in.

Might not like what I say, but

I pray that god feel me

and hears every word I say.

T.

A Daughter's Heart

Mama's eyes could tell secrets

reaching deep in within dead ends and deep down;

bottling the cans emptiness,

swallowing the cuts, leaving scars beyond digestive.

I watch you dry drown.

Arms opened wide.

Disconnected,

my shoulders lynched.

Heart aches from the headaches and sleepless nights

and mama's tears are mines,

at whole.

Piecing together what is still

broken;

steel

holding on to hope and I see you,

sometimes giving up;

a little girl rising from the inside/outgrowing the past that

still hunts steel hearts.

T.

20/01/03

In the last few years, I've come to face the card dealt. Coming to terms with heartbreaks and burned bridges. A lot has been said and done, and I take accountability for all the wrong I've chosen. But I realize that these decisions, most, were in the best interest of us both. Myself, first and foremost because toxin can cause more damage than a little bit and at some point, I felt like damaged goods. After being put down and held up by the ones I valued the most, I lost myself. I mean it's natural, it's within my spirit to love as hard as I do, but never again will I value love that is ungrateful. Even my family is not as deserving of my love as I would imagine growing up, but when cycles never change, it changes your character. Don't allow someone to slide because of the value you have held them to and don't allow that hurt to diminish your blessings or your happiness. Genuineness gravitates towards souls with the means to always hold love and compassion over all values. And as I become my own, I find myself cherishing the priceless moments instead. When I learned myself, I found true love.

T.

Autumn Leaves

Roses are red
 where the love and loyalty lie
between honesty
 and friendships
and families with good intentions.
 Where the bloody rivers that have flooded my people's
streets; in every hood
 the house holds the curse and it cycles for generations
streaming down my people's streets.

Violet becomes darker than blue
racism goes on forever, shots fired
and in every hood,
guns cocked and ready to let bodies pile like rocks on top
of potholes
and hearts repairing the love that left a void in their souls.
Tree roots hold together as the leaves fall with lost hopes,
holding the faith for our youth and the fate of our destiny.
These red roses are symbolic of the passion to keep
growing.

T.

A Million Cries

A thousand times I've heard of time healing all wounds and
I'm just waiting to be complete.
 Understanding that time has its way and the wheels just
keep moving.

Everything happens for a reason.
I take them lessons and discover that I can make it.
 These struggles being the barriers

of a climax at its highest
and we are just living in the moment
and planning for the future.

Mountains format at the peaks of success in small
packages. Growth is priceless,
amounting to more than just accomplishments. So then I
wonder what' really the right way? Do I listen to my mid or
my gut feeling, and when?
Frustration clouds my mind to the point where I black out
and flash. Speed off and crash, but I'm headed somewhere
and if that's another lesson, I just know I won't fold like
before.
I still have hope.
I shall fear not a soul and spirits are the more sacred to the
soul, so I stay aligned with myself and keep my foot on
their necks.

I'll give my breath if I have to.

I'll never give up.

My fate is stronger than any second thought I had to break through.

I keep telling myself, "Bitch you in your own way."

I can become my own setback.

And after a million cries, my tears have run dry. Flooding my insides so my headaches drown and the ambition in me walked the water of God's plan.

I keep my tears sacred though,

my most motivation is because of them nights under the covers balled up.

Them nights has become my greatest courage to embrace my struggles

to know what it feels like to be without and to never feel that again.

T.

Growth

There's a life awaiting to be reborn.

Young girl there's a voice within,

screaming green light.

It's go time

and it's time for you to release the wounds,

even the ones you refuse to open up

and those you meant to close, but never shut.

The curl patterns lock the water for this plant to grow,

this love to forever overpour and beyond this concrete

created,

through the waterfalls roses with melanin popping like

popcorn seeds under pressure,

rolling loud.

You could still hear the voice within,

on go,

whistling smoke that inhaled all doubts

and exhaled all the power of the tongue.

Using positive aspects to see through these disasters.

T.

She's like the Mississippi River,
easy going,
love overflowing,
but tensed.
Waves form in protection
for no nigga to disrespect this.
The root beneath all trees,
follicles rises beyond pores opening the center of her true
beauty that makes up
the makeup
without the powder
setting the foundation.
Her eyes shadow the crease aligning along her wings.
She's the caterpillar outgrowing her shell, keeping a smile
out of gratitude even when she suddenly feels stuck,
wanting to give up, holding on to love.
Life struck self love,
allowing these waters to rise as she confides in current
waves. Walls tighten along busted pipes, flooding the
minds of wandering thoughts. The sun rises up warm hearts
and sets on wine glasses, takes a sip of her puddles and
creates rainbows all night.

This is super Sunday after church. Her heartbeat sounds like the jazz band and moves the feet of others. Mentally locked in like Hurricane Katrina, she overcomes everything.

T.

For what it's worth, I am grateful for all the struggles I have faced thus far. All the cries shed, balled up under piles of screams, and steel built encouraged the things I value now. The dark nights with only a pot to piss in and a hotplate to eat off allowed me to experience a struggle I never want to feel again. Love, I never want to tolerate. Disrespect, I should never accept. You should never neglect yourself to satisfy another's need and desire if those aren't being returned, and it doesn't have to be exact, but what's expected is required to be given. Every day is a new opportunity for better results and greater strength. Your yesterday will never be today and tomorrow bringing something new. And for that, we should be grateful. Live in truth and treat people how you would want to be treated.

T.

Love Ran Dry

I became numb to your excuses of why you couldn't
comprehend my language of
screams and cries.
Five miscalls just to be ignored
when I only wanted to hear your voice,
 but you ignored me for the streets
 and they don't hear your calls.
 Who picks you up when you fall?
Repair the bones when your spine is broken,
back up
against the wall,
who you call?
 I broke into pieces trying to repair your pain and you took
that for granted.
Left my heart with another open wound,
 realizing this was a void I can only fulfil.
Realizing I was broken to begin with
 and I couldn't help you.
I couldn't love you.
I didn't love myself enough.
 I let your words tear me down
 so now I'm picking up those pieces I thought was lost.
 I became numb to your type of love and

being foolish.

I want more than Netflix and sex and something better than money.

Love is priceless, something you were afraid of and I almost gave up.

T.

When the Caged Bird Spoke

They say closed mouths don't get fed.

Fuck,

 a closed mind doesn't either.

Voices vain deep in thought;

gasping the possibility of rejection,

without taking a risk on the outcome.

Dreams start to fold like dry laundry

and with no guidance,

no knowledge;

no steppingstones to reach over the tip of the peek,

with shining slippers knocking together

wishing for dreams to come true,

leaves disappointments.

Shit like this is taught.

And when no one wanna step up,

when that voice in your head tells you to go get it and you

let up...

it's like a disease sickin' you

and life gets colder every blue moon,

it doesn't stop.

Them footsteps traveling behind you are gonna keep

traveling,

but it changes.

every moment, different.

Each experience…

forgive, but don't forget it.

They say fight for what's yours and claim it,

meaning self-respect,

gaining more and more.

Step into your purpose, allowing intuition to guide you.

Praying for better days as you step into another day,

thanking god for another chance.

Wearing a bulletproof vest with a "W" on your chest.

Not settling for less.

Hoping for the best.

We seek for miracles

like god's crying up a river for the flesh to drink,

but the mind is the miracle.

Pupils open wide

Focused on the reflecting image looking back at the quiet

sight of lips

shut solid. Soul

poking out trying to break the silence.

The big ass elephant hiding from the voices within yelling

for you to move into the light.

T.

Ice Breaks

Broad shoulders lean in

on comfort and sweet whispers of courage.

 Sacred lullabies sung of fears and dreams to conquer,

 the willpower to survive vicious hardships and I feel your

pain.

I understand your frustration.

 I admire your masculinity.

Our hearts are shaped in the hands of your mind, body, and

soul.

 Fist close, quick to defend thy honor that shall not be

disrespected.

 And I appreciate you.

Backs won't be the same without the spine you bring

to form this toughness for the passion

to stand firm and strengthen the strive to walk ahead.

 Rib cage the voices of deception that tried to

 or may have trapped you.

Digging holes only to find that the treasure was yours.

You are needed even when you feel unappreciated.

Beyond sex, a similar mindset is needed.

 Appreciate yourself

for being a human being and making a way when there
seems to be no way;
 for the throne you should hold yourself up to,
them long nights turning stars into moons. You shine.
 So, I shine even more when I see you smile.
 When you still try, and I appreciate your efforts.
 We shine
and everything feels so right when we feel alive
 and actually, be alive.
So, bald fist form
 to defend thy honor if they ever disrespect you.
Nonetheless should you ever be
 neglected, belittled, nor misdirected.
So, find yourself.
Take time to seek your truth and flaw,
 unhealed wounds and heal 'cause you deserve to.
 Unlearn some bad habits because you are supposed to.
You are black kings
so beautiful and knight,
bearing all the backlash from scars that were placed on
your backs.
Physically for our ancestors and
mentally in society.

Break down those barriers and pick up the pieces of
cracked teardrops
falling from faces just like you,
use that pain to water your outgrowing seeds and
change cycles.
 You are amazingly human.
And even though I can be impatient,
 I'll be patient with you

T.

Moments like this
forces me to reflect beyond the lines
eye peep.
Dilemmas within temptation repeats,
so, I deep
beyond these words I speak,
digging blueprints
with a little more sense of who I.
ten toes getting up, still
if I ever fall again.
Wrongs being right while righting my wrongs.
And with everything becoming a clone,
duplicating all sins,
blood bleeding bricks.
No time to be wasted.
No nigga worth it,
if he gotta be put before my patience.
No toleration for the bullshit, bitch.
Come correct or get to lacing.
I'm living, but I'm not living like you.
That's what makes us different.
We bleed the same, but

two different breeds.

Not your regular NOLA baby, this another level of crazy.

Hibernating in ink.

Tattooing vibrant energies so keep that negative shit from round me.

Bypassing the birds

Like crabs in a bucket trying to keep a bitch down.

I'm like fuck it

and fuck you too if you ain't fuckin with me.

Don't give attention to some shit that has no substance.

Trust issues making the love thin so bitch I'm a little more selfish with me.

T.

I am not just who I ought to be.

      I am a creation meant to soar.

            Baggy eyes so swollen,

           you'll think I never sleep,

               but nah,

             I weep for more.

      Like a lion in a jungle

with a heart of a ram,

in full force for adventure.

               I seek ambition.

With the courage to constantly mold myself into,

within use of nothing, but

    good vibes and persistent energies to keep

          my mind, body, and soul

      filled with positivity.

Thinking I am and will be

      cause the only way I shall not;

I cannot,

is if it's not meant for me.

      Ne-yo in my head like

        you a boss,

but sometimes I get the urge for some

lazy love.

Learned that lusting leaves room for child's play

And

thanks to porn, I learned my orgasm

so, I don't need a nigga for much.

Not just any man

has that magic touch to caress me,

perfectly

and I am to be respected,

pleased by any means.

Vice versa

cause nothing turns me on better than knowing my man is

taken care of.

I'm a queen, you're a king;

treat this as such.

A woman worth more

than what's in between the lips that clutch

that feeling that tingles.

Nah nigga, show me potential.

No perfection needed.

Definitely,

a woman that's worth a man that's about his.

Vice versa 'cause I can't look back,

Looking back at what has been done.

Looking back,

I reflect on my road ahead with these goals I then set.

I can't look back at how far I have come, looking back at who then and her now.

Flourishing into someone uniquely brilliant.

This woman's worth Promises to herself to never be broken again.

T.

There is a battle between loving yourself and loving others. It isn't selfish to choose you if others around you tend to be a stress in your life. You have to learn how to balance your health and your stability by controlling the energy you allow.

-Trell The Poet